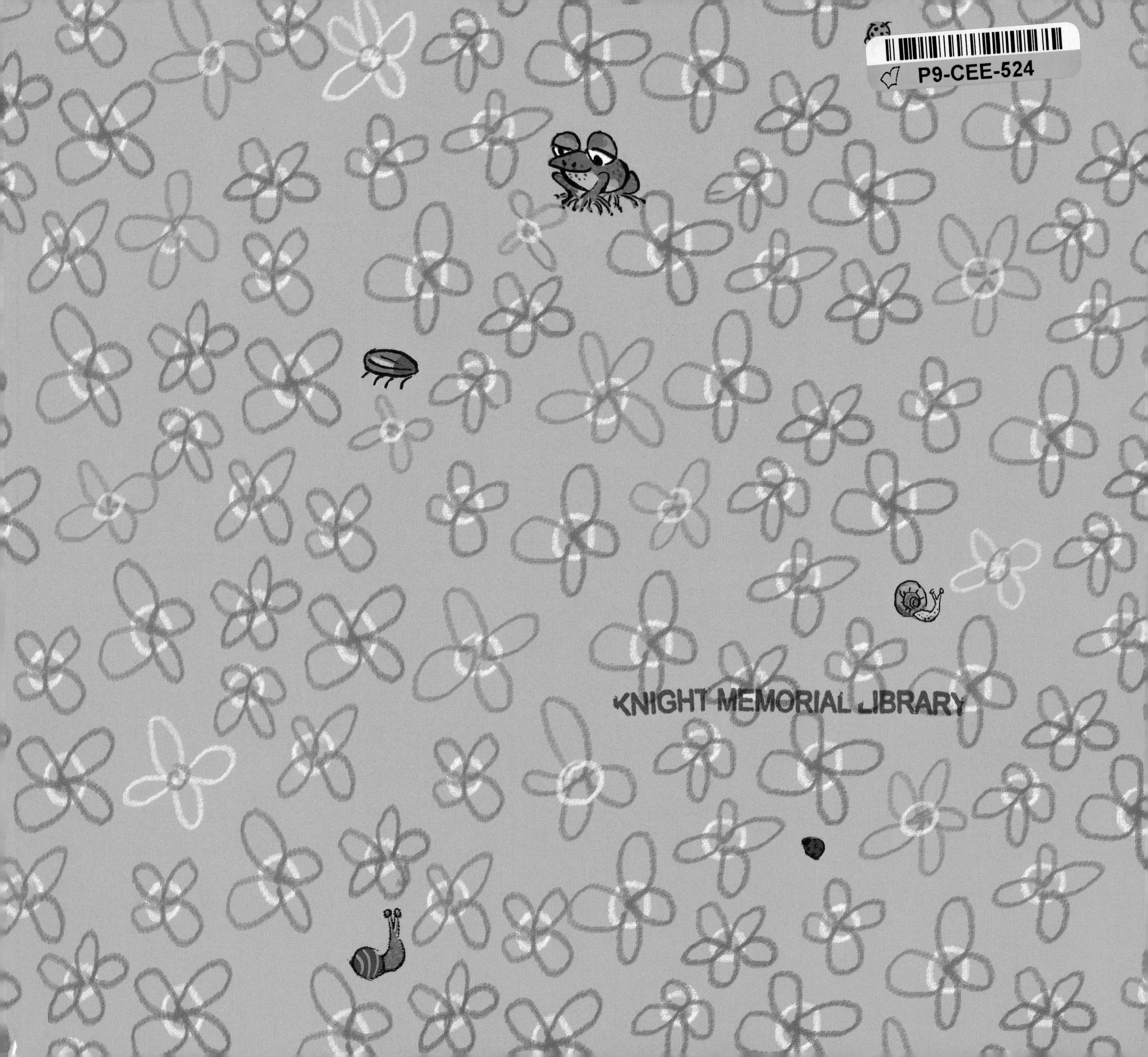

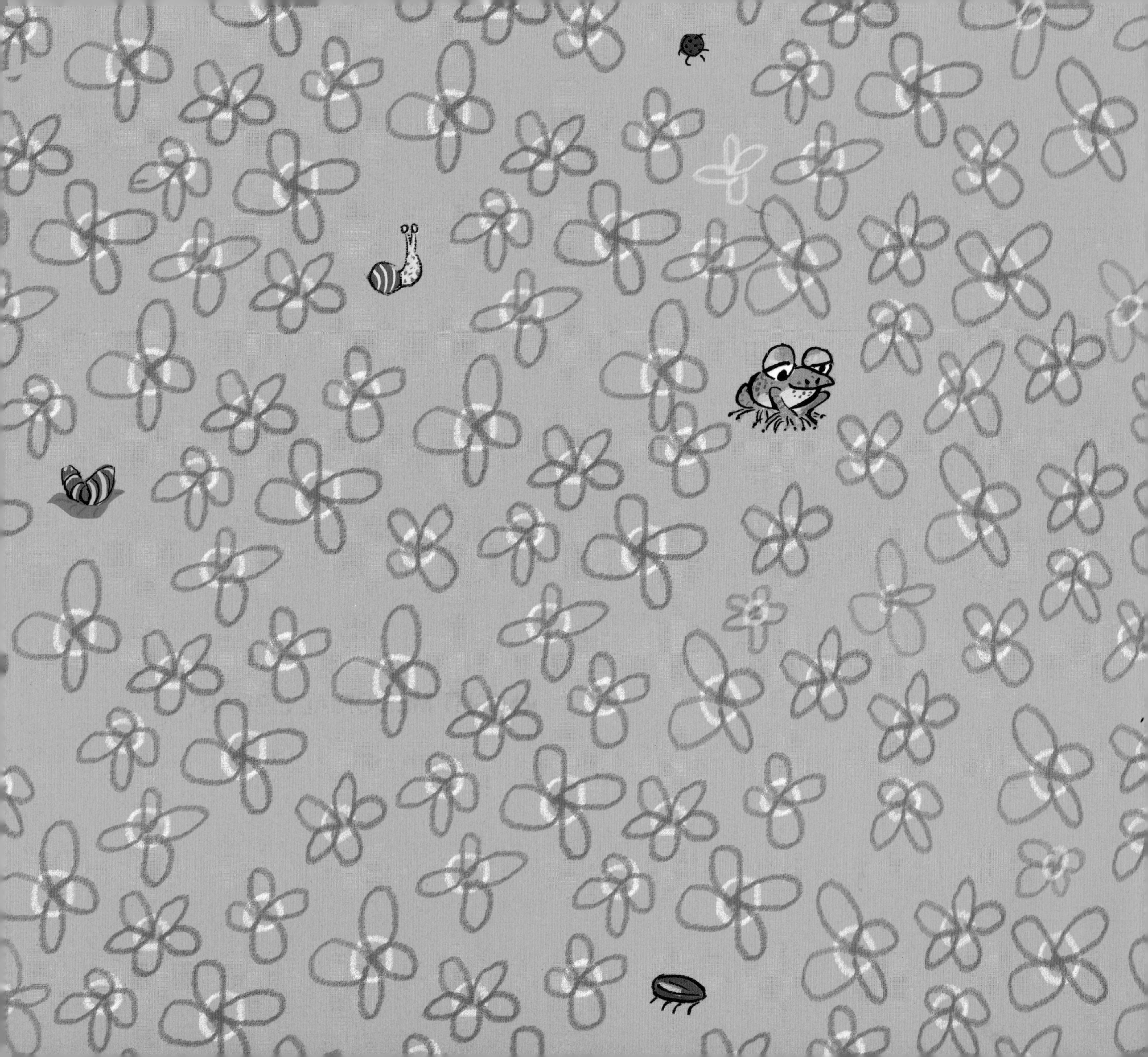

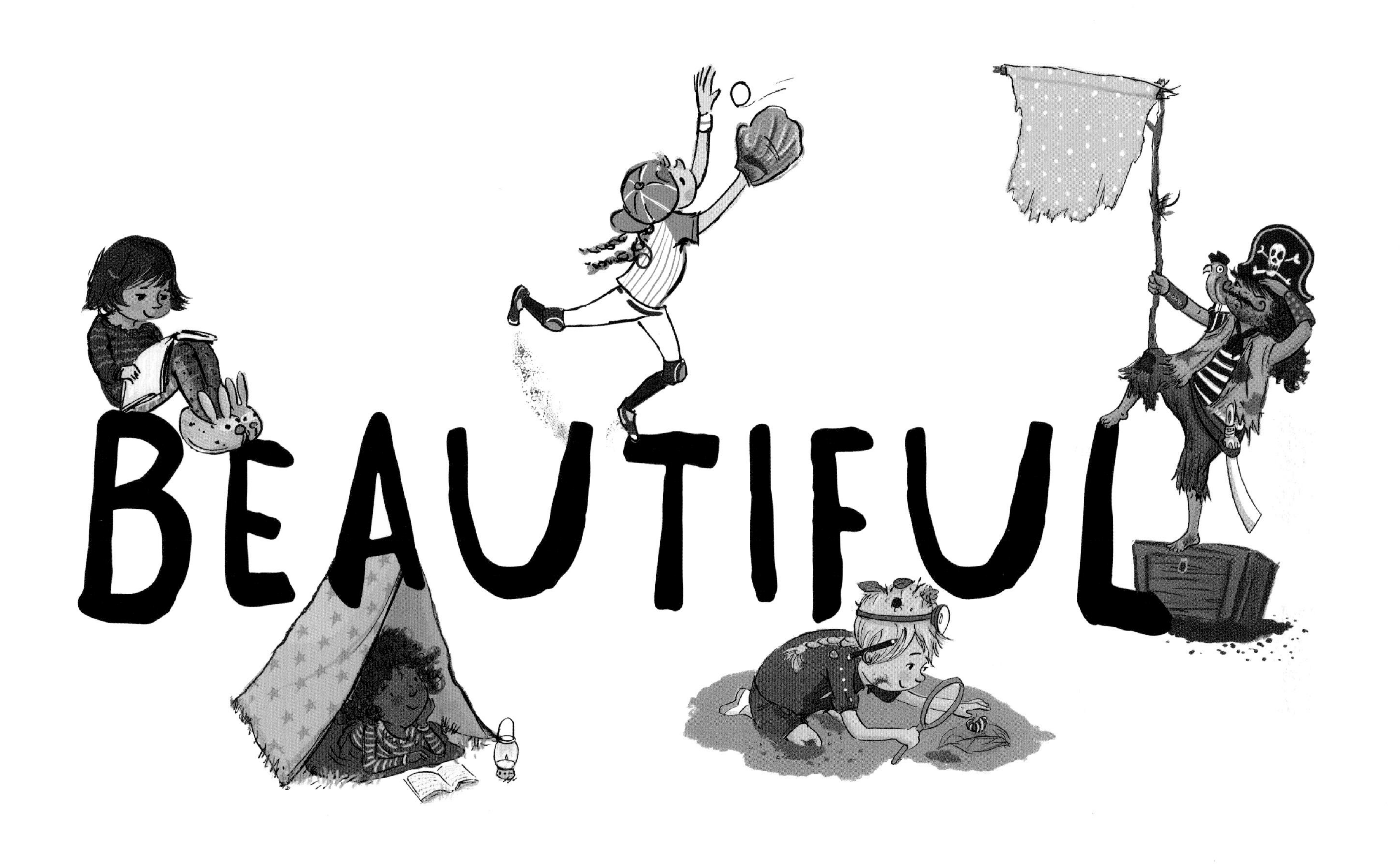

Stacy McAnulty

ILLUSTRATED BY

Joanne Lew-Vriethoff

Printed in China

ISBN 978-0-7624-5781-6
Library of Congress Control Number: 2015930721

9 8 7 6 5 4 3 2 1
Digit on the right indicates the number of this printing

Designed by T.L. Bonaddio
Edited by Lisa Cheng
Typography: Elsie, Close, and Daft Brush

Published by Running Press Kids
An Imprint of Running Press Book Publishers
A Member of the Perseus Books Group
2300 Chestnut Street
Philadelphia, PA 19103–4371

Visit us on the web!
www.runningpress.com/rpkids

For PAIGE and ELLERIE—AUNT STACY

For MAX WU YEN,
my baby girl, my inspiration—J.L.V.

Beautiful girls . . .

. . . have the perfect look.

Beautiful girls move gracefully.

And light up every room.

Beautiful girls know all about makeup.

BUGS

And have a smart style.

Beautiful girls smile sweetly.

And keep their hair properly in place.

Beautiful girls smell like flowers.

And sound like songbirds.

Beautiful girls love to look in the mirror.

And to spend time with beautiful people.

WOW!
STUNNING!

Beautiful girls deserve compliments.

100 Important Women in History
2x4=
4+4=
6+2

Because they make the world . . .

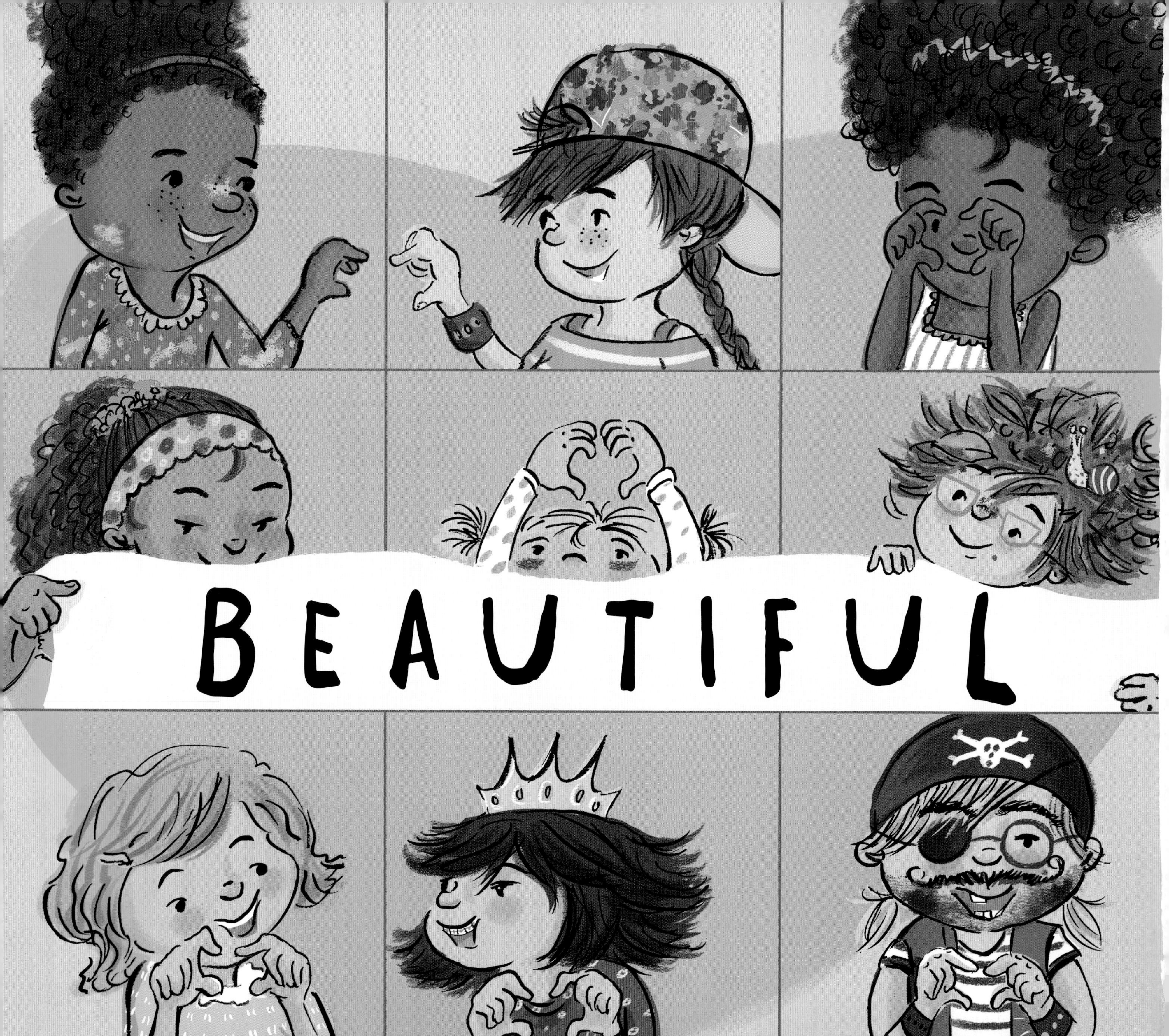
BEAUTIFUL

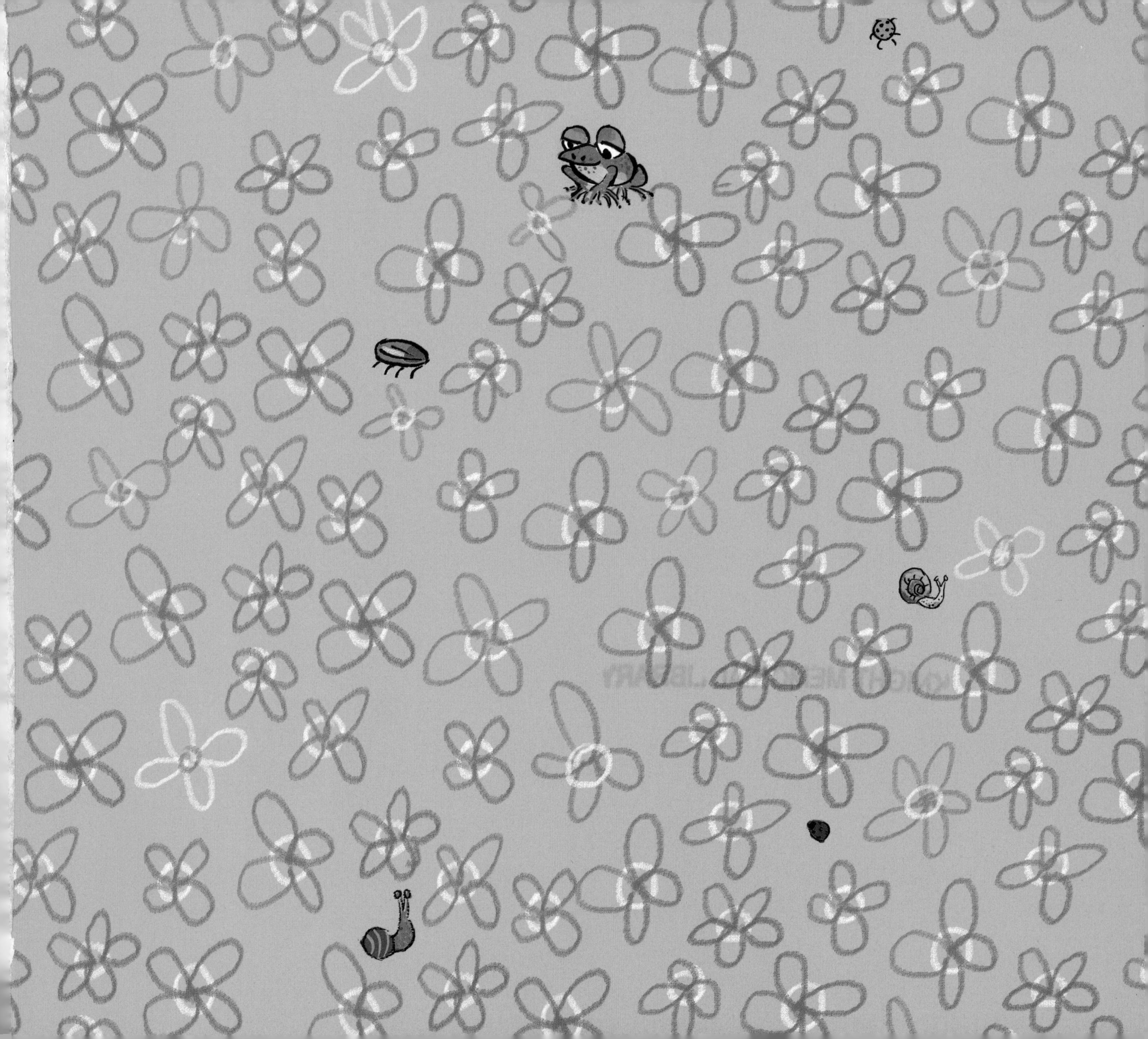

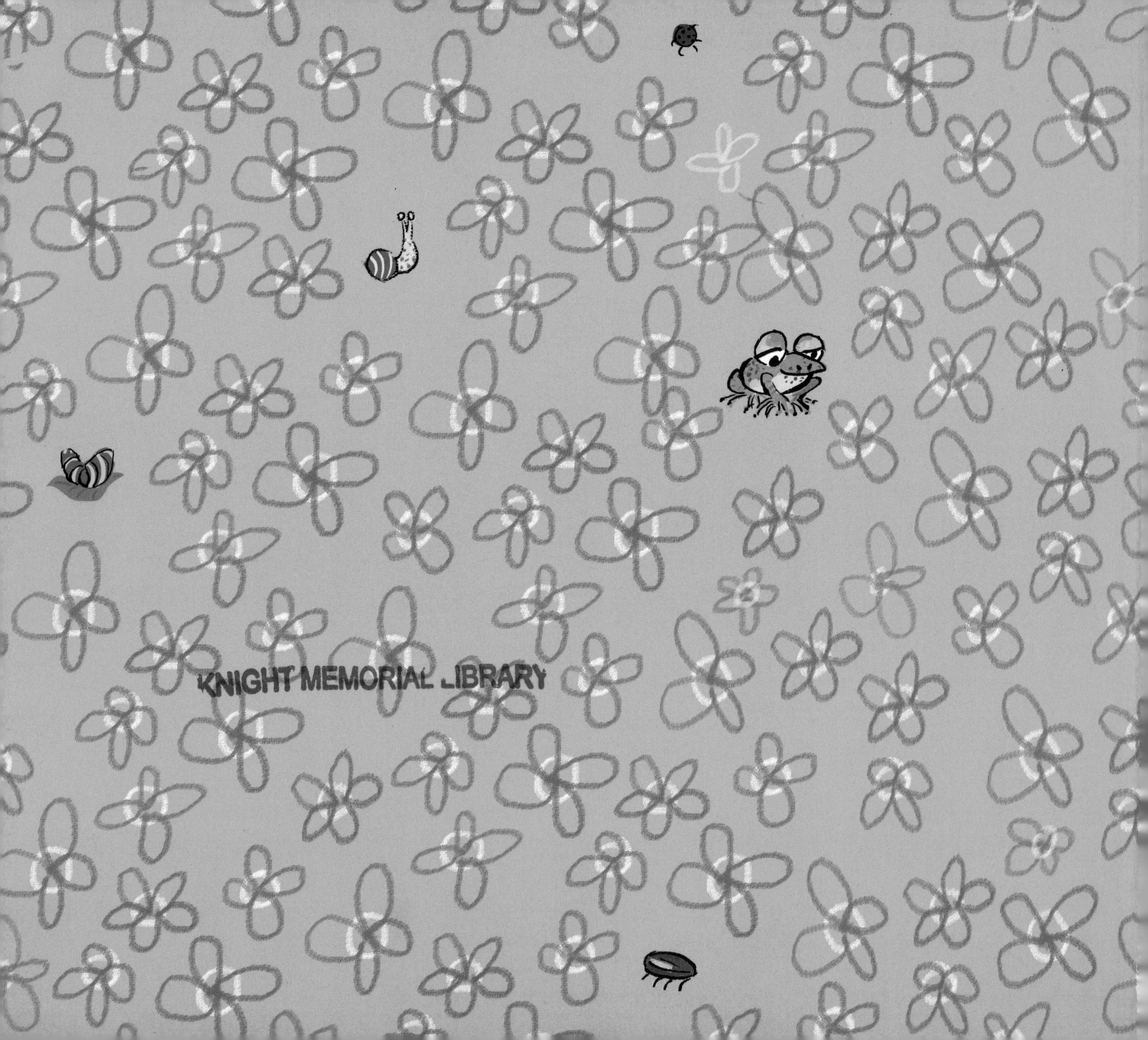